Sink It, Rusty

Illustrations by

Foster Caddell

SINK IT, RUSTY

by Matt Christopher

Little, Brown and Company

Boston • Toronto

LIBRARY OF CONGRESS CATALOG CARD NO. 63–13457

FIRST EDITION

*Published simultaneously in Canada
by Little, Brown & Company (Canada) Limited*

PRINTED IN THE UNITED STATES OF AMERICA

to

John and Ann

Sink It, Rusty

1

RUSTY YOUNG blew the whistle as hard as he could. The shrill sound pierced the big barn. It was so loud his own ears rang.

"Foul on Perry!" Rusty shouted.

"What?"

The boys on the floor stopped moving instantly. The tallest one stared at Rusty, his eyes cold and hard.

"You struck Joby's wrist when you stole the ball from him!" Rusty said. "I saw you!"

He trotted forward in his slow, awkward way, took the ball from Perry, and

3

handed it to Joby. "One shot," he said.

He felt Perry's stinging glance. Perry always thought he could get away with anything when he played basketball here with the kids. Probably he thought he could because he handled the ball better than any of them, and because he was the tallest.

Rusty didn't care. He'd call the fouls if he saw them, just like the referees did in the big games.

Joby stepped to the free-throw line. One of the boys had drawn it with white chalk a couple of weeks ago when the gang had first started coming to the barn to play basketball.

Joby held the ball close to his chest and looked long and hard at the basket. Players stood on each side of the free-throw lane, watching him. Rusty watched him, too. He could not help smiling a little. Every time Joby tried a foul shot, his mouth hung wide open.

Joby shot. The ball hit the backboard, bounced back and fluttered through the net.

"Nice shot!" somebody yelled.

Joby's mouth snapped shut like a trap and he grinned.

Jim Bush caught the ball as it dropped from the basket. He stepped near the wall at one side of the backboard, passed the ball to Perry. Perry dribbled it down-court.

Rusty followed him. For a moment he tried to keep up with Perry. Then he slowed down. His legs refused to obey his wishes. He couldn't lift his knees as high as he wanted to. He couldn't take long strides.

That was why he was refereeing now instead of playing.

Mom and Dad said he was improving, though. He wished he could improve faster. He wanted to play basketball as well as the boys did. And other sports, too.

Mom and Dad had often reminded him that he was much more fortunate than many other children. Some had serious effects from polio for years and years, whereas he had got over the worst of his two years ago.

Two years! And he still wasn't able to run, jump, and do other things that his friends did!

Rusty pushed the thoughts from his mind. He watched Perry dribble toward the basket. Corny Moon was guarding Perry closely. Quick as a wink, Perry dribbled past him and broke for the basket. He went up, pushed the ball against the backboard, and scored two points.

The ball dropped to the floor. Rusty caught it on the bounce. He tossed it to a boy waiting to take it out. Then he saw a movement near the corner of the room, and paused to get a better look.

A man had climbed the ladder from the floor below. He wasn't really too old — perhaps twenty-five. But boy, was he tall! Six-foot-four! That's what the kids had said. His name was Alec Daws. His father had recently purchased the grocery store in Cannerville. They were still a little like strangers.

He stepped onto the floor. A wide grin spread across his face.

"Keep playing," he said. "Don't stop because of me."

For a second Rusty's gaze fell upon the

black glove Alec Daws wore on his left hand. He thought it was funny that Alec should wear only one glove.

The boys played awhile longer. Rusty blew the whistle a couple of times when he thought a foul was made. Both times the boys on whom Rusty made the call yelled at him. And both times Rusty's face turned red.

"Here, Mr. Daws," he said, holding the ball out toward the tall onlooker. "You ref."

"No. You're doing all right," said Alec Daws.

"Good idea!" Perry Webb exclaimed. "Come on, Alec! Ref for us!"

Alec Daws smiled, shrugged, and accepted the ball from Rusty.

Rusty went to the side of the floor and sat down. The boys played more carefully

now that Alec was refereeing. But while Rusty watched, an ache started inside him. An ache to be on the floor, to run. An ache to scramble after the ball, to dribble it, and to shoot for the basket.

After a while, when the action was taking place near the farther basket, he went to the ladder and climbed down.

He was glad nobody was around to see his face when he reached the bottom.

2

RUSTY walked across the cracked cement floor toward the wide, open doorway. Overhead, the boards squeaked from running, thumping feet.

He walked outside into the cool night air. A high moon hung like a glowing crystal ball in the sky. It was about seven o'clock. Mom and Dad expected him home soon, anyway.

He got to thinking about his future. It looked very dim. Alec Daws had taken interest in the boys' playing basketball. He would be coming to the barn more often now. No doubt he understood the game well. At least, well enough to know how to referee.

All at once Rusty didn't like Alec Daws. He didn't like him at all. Alec had come and taken away from him the one thing he was able to do — referee.

The evening was so quiet Rusty could hear the soft whisper of the creek water to his left. He walked alongside the concrete wall and watched the moonlit water glisten like patches of silver. He reached the bridge, crossed it, and started down the paved road.

On the right was a park. Picnic benches stood empty under shadowy trees. Beyond the park was Cato Lake, a dark-blue mirror under the pale moon.

Ahead, on the left, was the Dawses'

grocery store. A dim, yellow light beamed out from its big window. The store was closed.

Rusty looked up at the hill behind the store. It was steep, covered with pine trees, elms, and oaks. On top of the hill he could see the outline of a house. Other houses were up there, out of his view. One of them was his.

Rusty paused. He could continue on his way home by taking the road. It led past the store, wound around the hill and up to the houses. But now he wanted to take the shortcut. He would climb the steep hill.

He walked behind the store, reached the bottom of the hill, and began climbing. He discovered that the dark tree-shadows made it hard to see. The footing was difficult, too. The ground was hard as rock.

He slipped on dead leaves and clutched a tiny sapling to keep from falling. He helped himself upward by pulling on the saplings. By the time he was a third of the way up the hill his legs ached. His arms were tired. He wished now he had taken the road.

Suddenly, he slipped again. He reached out in the darkness for a sapling or some brush to stop his fall. He grabbed at a thin branch. But he fell so quickly that the branch slid through his hand. He rolled down the hill, panic filling his heart. Twigs snapped loudly as he rolled over them.

Finally, he struck the wide base of a tree. He lay still a moment, breathing hard.

His breathing was the only sound he heard in the very still night. He shuddered and wondered if he was hurt.

3

RUSTY got up. He wasn't hurt. He brushed the dirt off his clothes. He swallowed and pressed his lips tightly together.

Just then a voice from the direction of the barn broke the stillness of the night.

"Rusty! Rusty! Wait for me!"

Joby's voice.

"I'm up here, Joby," he replied. "Wait! I'm coming down."

He could see Joby running swiftly toward the bridge. Carefully, Rusty climbed down the hill. He reached the bottom and walked out of the shadows. Joby came running toward him.

"Rusty!" he shouted. "What were you doing up there?"

"I wanted to take the shortcut," said Rusty, ashamed. "Nobody else ever had trouble climbing that hill."

"But it's night!" said Joby. "It's hard to see."

"I know," replied Rusty. "Guess that's why I fell. If it hadn't been for a tree, I might have rolled all the way to the bottom."

"You fell?" Joby's voice pierced the night air. "You sure were nutty trying to climb that hill! Come on. Let's take the road. I'm going home, too."

They walked to the paved road and followed it around the hill. Lights on poles blazed the way.

"Joby," said Rusty suddenly, "please don't tell anybody I tried to climb the hill."

"Don't worry," said Joby. "I won't. But you were really nutty to do it!"

They reached the houses on top of the hill. Lights glowed in windows. Smoke curled out of chimneys, faded into the dark sky.

Joby's and Rusty's homes were across from each other.

"Goodnight, Joby," said Rusty.

"Goodnight, Rusty."

The instant Rusty walked into the kitchen he looked at his pants. Horror came over him. They were covered with dirt! There were even bits of twigs and leaves sticking to his clothes.

Quickly, he began brushing them off. But he wasn't improving things. The dirt was bouncing onto the clean, polished floor. If Mom —

He started to go back out. Just then his mother appeared from the dining room.

"Rusty! Heavens! What are you doing? And where in glory's name have you been?"

Rusty trembled and stammered out his story.

Her blue eyes softened. Rusty hoped she'd smile, too, but she didn't.

"Get the clothes brush, step outside, and get yourself cleaned," she ordered. "And then sweep up this floor. After that, you'd better take a bath."

Rusty did all those things. Afterwards, his mother showed him a letter they had received from Marylou, Rusty's sister. She was a sophomore at State Teachers College.

He read the letter. There were a lot of words, but as far as Rusty was concerned she hardly said anything.

Rusty didn't go to the barn again until Saturday afternoon. First he made sure no one was there. He took his own basketball and began playing all by himself.

He dribbled and shot from different spots on the floor. His shots were either too short or far to the left or right of the basket. He tried jump shots and realized he could hardly get off the floor.

Anger built up inside him. Why couldn't he run faster? Why couldn't he jump? Why did he have to be different from other boys? *Why did it have to happen to him?*

"Hello!" a voice said behind him.

He dropped the ball. He spun, and almost lost his balance.

"Oh! Hi!" he said. His heart thumped. "Hi, Mr. Daws!"

4

"I saw you pass by the store with the basketball," said Alec. "I thought you were coming here. Practicing shots?"

"I guess so," said Rusty.

Alec came forward. He walked gracefully despite his towering height. A smile warmed his gray eyes. Then a little frown appeared on his forehead.

"Aren't you the boy who was refereeing the ball game here a few nights ago?"

Rusty nodded. He was really nervous. Boy, this guy was tall!

"Bet you didn't like it when I took over your job, did you?" Alec Daws said.

Rusty looked away. He shrugged. "I —
I didn't mind," he said.

Alec Daws reached out a long, muscu-
lar arm and squeezed Rusty's shoulder.
"Don't tell me that," he said. "What's your
name? Mine's Alec Daws. You can call me
Alec."

"My name's Ronald Young," said Rusty.
"Everybody calls me Rusty. Because of
my hair."

Alec laughed.

Rusty's gaze fell upon the black glove
Alec wore on his left hand. There was
something strange about the hand. Even
with the glove on, it didn't look as big as
the other.

"Go ahead," said Alec. "Let's see you hit
one from here."

Rusty turned, looked at the basket. He

stood near the middle of the floor. He had no chance of even hitting the backboard from here. He began to dribble, then quickly stopped. He stood frozen, his face turning red.

"What's the matter, Rusty?"

"N-nothing," he said. He shot. The ball fell far short.

He'll notice something is wrong with my legs! He will!

Suddenly Alec swept past him. He caught the bouncing ball with one hand — the hand without the glove — and dribbled it to the side. He stopped, held the ball up in both hands, then shot at the basket. Rusty noticed that Alec had used his gloved hand only to hold the ball up in front of him. When he shot, he used only his right hand.

The ball arched beautifully, and sank through the hoop.

Rusty stared. What a shot!

"Now you try it, Rusty," Alec said. He caught the ball and tossed it to Rusty.

Rusty dribbled slowly toward the basket, then stopped and looped a shot. The ball banged against the rim and dropped to the floor.

"Run after it!" said Alec.

Rusty ran after it. He tried hard to lift his knees, to keep from scraping the toes of his sneakers. He felt the ache in his legs, felt his toes scrape the floor, and knew he wasn't succeeding. He reached the ball, tried to make a quick shot, and stumbled. He fell. Once more his face flushed.

Alec rushed toward him, picked him up, and grinned.

"Hurt yourself?"

"No," said Rusty. "Guess I'm — slow."

"Just take it easy," said Alec. "You rushed the ball too fast. I have a suggestion. Go over to that corner. Inside the playing area."

Rusty went to the corner. Alec bounced the ball to him.

"Shoot," said Alec, "then chase after the ball, and shoot from the opposite side."

Rusty shot. He missed, went after the ball, and shot it from the other corner.

"Make that your goal," said Alec. "Every time you come here, practice those corner shots. You'll start hitting, and some day you'll be a corner-shot artist."

Rusty grinned. "Okay," he said.

He and Alec took turns shooting at the basket. Rusty saw how gracefully Alec moved, how quickly he dribbled, how smoothly he made his lay-ups.

"Did you ever play on a team, Alec?" Rusty asked.

"In high school and college," said Alec. "Until I hurt my hand."

Rusty's eyes widened. "Hurt your hand playing basketball?"

"Oh, no. I worked on a farm during my summer vacation a few years ago, and did it on a corn husker. That finished me." Alec stood near the middle of the court now. He aimed for the basket and shot. The ball hit the backboard and bounced into the net.

"I had polio," Rusty said. "That's why I can't move around very fast."

"I figured that," said Alec. "You'll come along fine, though. Best thing in the world is exercise." He took another shot, then headed for the ladder. "Well, I must get back to the store. Keep shooting, Rusty!"

29

"Thanks for coming, Alec!" Rusty said.

Five minutes after Alec left, Corny Moon and Perry Webb showed up.

"Well, look who's here!" cried Perry. "What are you doing, Rusty?"

"Practicing corner shots," replied Rusty. "Alec Daws was just here. He told me to keep at it and maybe I'll become a corner-shot artist."

Perry and Corny laughed. Rusty could tell that laugh. They thought it was really funny.

His lips tightened. He took his ball and started down the ladder.

"Wait!" said Perry. "We're sorry, Rusty. We didn't mean to be nasty."

"Stick around," added Corny. "Let's the three of us play awhile."

Rusty paused, then changed his mind. Well, guess they didn't *really* mean it.

30

They took turns shooting at the basket. Rusty's shots seldom hit. But he did as Alec had suggested. He kept shooting from the corners. Perhaps someday he might become good at it.

Perhaps.

5

"**D**ID Alec tell you he's going to buy uniforms and form a basketball team?" said Perry.

Rusty was holding the ball, ready to shoot. Now he looked at Perry wonderingly.

"No. Alec didn't say anything to me about it."

That was funny, he thought. *Why didn't Alec say something to me about it?*

"Come on, Rusty!" yelled Corny. "Let go of the ball!"

Rusty shot. He threw far short. Corny

caught the ball on a bounce, broke fast for the basket, and laid it up neatly.

"He's going to get games for us," went on Perry excitedly, as he dashed after the bouncing ball. "Boy, will that be fun!"

I wonder, thought Rusty. *I wonder if I will get a uniform.*

Rusty thought a lot about that afterwards.

Monday, in gym class, Rusty worked out with the other boys. For a while Mr. Jackson, the gym teacher, let the boys do as they wished. Some got on the trampoline, some on the "horse." Others got on the bars and chinned themselves. After they limbered their bodies, Mr. Jackson explained what their program was for this period.

He had them spread out in orderly fashion on the floor. Then he led them through a series of exercises — situps, knee bends, and jumping jacks.

Rusty tried to do them as well as he was able, but he could not sit up and touch his toes as so many other boys could. He also had trouble bending his knees.

Mr. Jackson looked at him often and smiled encouragingly.

"Okay! Rest a bit!" said Mr. Jackson finally.

Rusty perspired freely. He breathed hard. He was glad to rest. Mr. Jackson approached him. He was short, with blond, wavy hair and very blue eyes.

"Feel okay, Rusty?" he asked.

"Just a little tired," said Rusty.

"I'm going to have the boys sprint," said Mr. Jackson. "You don't have to join them if you don't want to."

"I think I will, though, Mr. Jackson,"

said Rusty. "If it's all right with you."

"Of course," said the gym teacher, and patted Rusty gingerly on the shoulder.

He's sorry for me. I don't want him to be sorry for me! I don't want anybody to be sorry for me!

He sprinted with the boys, and came in far behind. Some looked at him, smiling. Most of them paid him no attention. Rusty's coming in last wasn't news to them.

On Wednesday evening, Joby stopped for Rusty. Both walked down the hill to the barn, wearing warm winter jackets and hats. The evening air was biting cold. Below them, Lake Cato was like blue glass.

Only three boys were at the barn when Joby and Rusty arrived. Within fifteen minutes all the boys who had been coming regularly to play basketball were present. They were playing with Corny Moon's basketball — the same one they always played with.

Time and time again Rusty tried to get the ball and shoot. Always someone would break in front of him, take the ball, and dribble it away.

Finally, Joby got it and tossed it to him. Later, Ted Stone passed it to him. Both times he dribbled the ball to one of the corners and shot. After a while he got so discouraged that he didn't try to get the ball any more.

Presently, Joby Main yelled out: "Perry! Heard any more about Alec's forming a team? Who's going to buy the uniforms?"

At once everyone stopped running. Corny had the ball. He tucked it under his arm. Everybody looked at Perry Webb.

"He's going to buy the uniforms himself," replied Perry. "He's going to get games with teams from other towns. Soon, I guess. Of course, he's going to pick only the best players. Whoever doesn't show for practice won't play."

His eyes met Rusty's. "Players got to be real good, too," Perry went on. "I don't think you'd make the team, Rusty. I know it's tough not to play. But I'm sure Alec won't — well, I think it's just impossible for you to be on the team, Rusty."

6

JOBY, Corny, and Rusty walked up the road between the two rows of houses that Saturday morning. The cold December air reddened their cheeks. A beagle came out and greeted them silently. They saw no one else. It was either too cold or too early in the morning for people to be out.

They soon left the houses behind them. Joby turned off the road and headed into the woods. Corny and Rusty trailed after him. They were going to check Joby's traps. He had six of them set in different parts of the woods.

"How far is the first one?" Rusty asked.

"Not far," said Joby. "About a quarter of a mile."

"A quarter of a mile?" Rusty echoed. "Jeepers!"

Joby laughed. "Sounds far but it isn't."

They weaved around trees and stumps. The trees were thick here. They were mostly elms and evergreens. Rusty saw a nest dangling beneath the branch of one of the elms. It pleased him to know that it was an oriole's nest.

"Hey! Look at that!" whispered Corny.

A pair of squirrels were standing, face down, on the side of an elm. Their bushy tails were curled up behind them. As the boys approached them, the little furred animals whisked around, darted up the tree, and disappeared.

The boys chuckled happily. Rusty began to enjoy this trip into the woods. He had gone on short hikes with his father. But he had never gone deep into the woods.

It was quiet now, too, except for the chirping of birds and the chittering noises of squirrels. There was a fresh smell of leaves, of tree bark. He spotted a tiny rabbit. What a nice pet that little fellow would make!

Suddenly Rusty discovered he was alone. He was so slow he had fallen behind. He shouldn't have been looking for animals nor listening for their sounds.

Panic gripped him a moment.

"Joby! Corny!" he shouted. "Where are you?"

From a short distance ahead of him, Rusty heard them reply. "Right here, Rusty!"

He hurried and caught up with them. He panted. Even though the air was bitter cold, his face was hot as fire.

"Here's the first trap," said Joby at last.

It was near the entrance of a wide hole in the ground. Leaves were spread over it. It wasn't sprung.

"That's a weasel hole," said Joby. "Dad says weasels are hard to catch. I believe it!"

He led Corny and Rusty to three other traps. One was snapped. Joby looked at it excitedly, but whatever had snapped it wasn't around now.

"That's a raccoon hole," explained Joby. "Dad told me that snapping a trap is a favorite trick of a coon's. I'll keep after him, though, until I catch him."

Rusty laughed. "Maybe he'll forget to play tricks some day."

"I hope!" said Joby.

He opened the jaws of the trap again, set it, and placed it near the mouth of the hole. Then he carefully covered it with leaves.

"I'll be back tomorrow, Mr. Coon!" he said.

They walked on. Soon Rusty heard the rippling waters of a creek. A few moments later they arrived at its bank. The water was shallow. Rusty saw no place where they could walk across, except a log stretched over the creek like a bridge.

Rusty stared as Joby and Corny walked on it to the other side. He got on it, took three steps, then stopped.

"Come on, Rusty!" yelled Joby. "You can make it!"

He took another step, then looked along the log. It wasn't very big around. Some of

its bark had been stripped off. There was about six feet of space between it and the water underneath. If he slipped —

Rusty shuddered and backed off. Joby and Corny laughed.

I'll try it on my knees, he thought.

He got down on his knees, crawled about five feet, and paused. He stared at the water, got a little dizzy, and closed his eyes tightly. He opened them again. Without looking over the side of the log, he backed off.

Joby and Corny laughed again. "There's a place a little farther down you can walk across, Rusty," yelled Joby.

Rusty cracked a weak grin. "I'll take it!" he said.

He found the place. The creek was wider here. The water flowed in a lot of tiny rivers. There were spots of green, slippery moss, but Rusty walked across without trouble.

Joby led them to another trap.

"Hey! Look at this!" he cried excitedly.

There sat a rabbit. At the sound of Joby's voice it hopped around a little. It didn't get anywhere. One of its hind feet was caught in the trap.

The three boys stared at it in silence. Then they looked at each other.

Neither one of them moved for a long, long minute.

7

"FIND me a club," said Joby.

Corny searched for one. He found a broken branch about two feet long. He handed it to Joby.

Joby took it. He looked at the club, and then at the rabbit. The rabbit was sitting still, its eyes big and wide.

Joby shook his head, and handed the club to Corny. "Here, you do it," he said.

Corny took the club. He lifted it. The rabbit had not moved a bit.

Corny lowered the club. "Here. You do it, Rusty," he said.

Rusty took the club. He looked at the

rabbit. The tip of its short tail looked like a ball of cotton.

"Not me. I can never do it," said Rusty. He flung the club away.

Joby crouched beside the animal, opened the trap, and the rabbit hopped away on its three good legs.

"His leg will heal," said Joby. There was kind of a joy in his voice, as if it made him happy to let the rabbit loose.

Rusty and Corny both smiled.

"Come on!" said Joby. "There's one more trap left!"

Joby led them to the shore of the creek. The trap was set near the water, with half of an apple on it for bait. The bait had not lured any animal, though. The trap was still unsprung.

"Well, that's it," said Joby. "Zero average. But I still think it's fun to trap!"

"Me, too!" said Rusty.

"You did catch a rabbit," Corny reminded him.

"Yeah," smiled Joby. "But rabbits are different. You can't kill them. They're like pets. You wouldn't kill your pet dog, would you?"

" 'Course not," said Corny.

They retraced their steps through the woods, and went back home. Rusty knew he'd remember that trip for a long, long time.

He'd remember that log, too.

Later, from the window of his living room, Rusty saw Perry Webb, Corny, Ted Stone, and several other boys walking down the road. Corny was carrying his basketball. As the boys passed in front of

Rusty's house, Corny looked at the house. He said something to Perry. Perry shook his head, *no*.

Corny wanted to ask me to go with them. But Perry doesn't want me to. A lump rose in Rusty's throat.

A little while later Rusty got his own basketball and went outside. Dad had made a backboard above the garage door. Rusty practiced shooting long shots. He tried hard not to think of Perry and the others.

He practiced until his legs got tired. Then he went inside to rest. Sometime later he saw the boys returning. He could hear them chattering excitedly among themselves. Each was carrying a small bundle of blue and red under his arm.

Rusty knew what those bundles were.

They were suits — basketball suits. Alec Daws had passed them out.

Rusty turned, stretched out full length on the easy chair, and gazed at his legs. They looked the same as anybody else's. But they were weak, slow.

Why did it have to be me?

"What's the matter, son?"

Rusty looked up. Dad was in the doorway, a tall man with dark hair and wide shoulders. His brown eyes were understanding.

"Nothing," said Rusty.

"Nothing?" Dad chuckled. "I saw those boys walking up the street. They were carrying basketball suits, weren't they?"

Rusty shrugged. "I guess so," he said.

"I think they were," said Dad. "I heard the fathers talking about it in the store.

51

Alec Daws is going to buy suits and form a basketball team. I think it's a wonderful idea. Good for the boys. Why didn't you go down and get your suit?"

Rusty looked at his father squarely. "Me? I can't make the team, Dad!"

"Oh?" Dad's brows lifted. "Who said you can't?"

Rusty put his elbow on the arm of the chair, sank his chin into the palm of his hand hopelessly. "I just know I can't," he said.

"You might be fooling yourself," said Dad. "Alec is a pretty square shooter. He's not trying to form a team of champions. He just wants a team. He wants to make it as good as he can, but he's not going to keep kids off who want to play. I've met Alec. He's a nice, decent guy."

"I know," said Rusty. "I met him, too."

He put on his jacket, got his basketball, and went outside again. Even when his legs got tired, he didn't quit. He grew awfully hungry, too. But he still played.

Presently small flakes of snow fell. The flakes grew larger and began to stick to the ground. They fell on his cheeks, melting instantly. Still Rusty played, working on corner shots. He was sinking them better as the minutes dragged on.

Patches of white formed on the ground. Rusty moved about much more slowly now. He didn't run after the ball when he shot. He walked. He wanted to stay out as long as he could.

"Rusty, you've been out there for hours!" Mom's voice suddenly broke the silence around him. "Come into the house!"

"Okay, Mom!" he said.

He picked up his basketball, went in. He took off his coat and hat, dropped into a living room chair, and fell sound asleep.

8

DURING lunch hour on Monday, Perry Webb ran up behind Rusty in the hall.

"Hi, Rusty. Heard you're afraid of logs."

Rusty whirled. "Logs? What logs?"

Perry laughed. "You know what I'm talking about. You went along with Joby and Corny last Saturday, didn't you? You came to a log. They walked across it, but you didn't!"

Rusty blushed. "Oh, that," he said.

Two other boys met him in the hall. They laughed and mentioned the log, too.

A knot formed in Rusty's stomach. He

walked faster, hoping to get away from the boys. They walked faster, too.

Rusty reached the end of the hall, turned right and started down the stairs. Suddenly, he stopped. Coming up were Joby and Corny.

His eyes blurred as they bored into theirs.

"You — you told them!" he said angrily.

Joby's eyes widened. "Told them what?"

"You know what!" Rusty's voice rose sharply.

"Oh, forget it," said Perry. "We were only kidding, Rusty. We didn't mean to hurt you."

Rusty's gaze swung to Corny. Corny's face paled. "It was me, Rusty. I told them. But I didn't know they would —"

Rusty didn't wait for Corny to finish. He fled down the stairs as fast as he could.

He stumbled, gripped the banister tightly, caught himself, and went on. He entered the gym and sat down, his heart pounding fiercely. He watched a scrub basketball game until the bell rang.

That afternoon, Rusty climbed off the bus in front of the Daws Grocery Store. He saw Alec carrying a garbage can around the side of the building. Perry, Corny, and the others stopped and spoke to the tall coach of their new team. Rusty heard them speak about their new uniforms, but he hurried past as if he didn't see Alec. Alec wasn't interested in him, anyway.

"Rusty! Wait a minute!"

Rusty turned.

Alec winked at him. "Be at the barn about six," he said. "Can I count on you?"

Rusty looked at Perry, Corny, Joby, and

the others who were regular players at the barn. They looked back at him as if they didn't quite believe that Alec would invite *him*, Rusty.

"Okay," he said. He turned, and continued home by himself.

That night, at six o'clock, Alec Daws gave Rusty his uniform. It had a number 6 on the jersey.

"I had it for you last Saturday," Alec said. "I was sure you'd like to have one."

The lump in Rusty's throat was as big as a baseball. "I — I sure did!" he whispered.

"Be here for practice with the rest of the boys every night this week," went on Alec. "I arranged a game this Saturday with the Benton Braves, a non-league team. Later on, there will be more. All

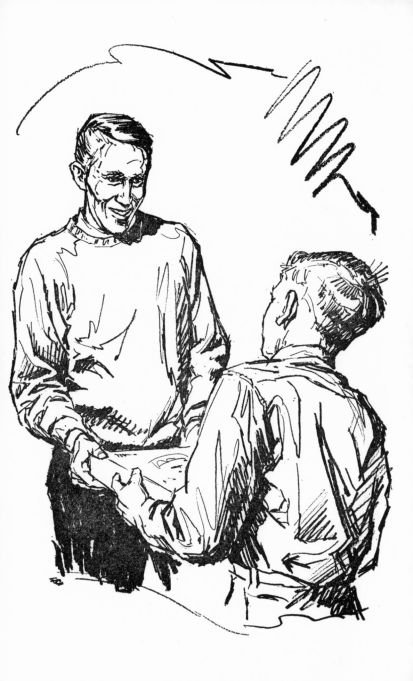

right. Put that suit aside for now. I want you to get on the B team."

Rusty saw that members of the A team were Joby Main and Mark Andrews at the forward positions, Corny Moon and Bud Farris at the guard positions, and Perry Webb at center.

For five minutes the A team showed strong power over the B team. Perry racked up three baskets himself, and Bud made one. The B team didn't get any.

Alec exchanged some of the players to make the teams better balanced. This appealed to the boys. Rusty didn't enter into the scrambles for the ball. He'd never have a chance, he thought. He played the corner, as Alec had told him to do.

But that evening he didn't sink a shot.

Just before the boys left for home, Alec

had them choose a name for their new team.

They decided on "The Lakers."

When game time arrived Saturday afternoon, Rusty was certain that Alec would not let him play. All he had sunk during that week of basketball practice were two baskets for a total of four points.

Several fathers drove their cars to the game at Benton, four miles away from Cannerville. The Lakers looked sharp and eager in their blue and red uniforms. The Benton Braves were flashy in their green ones.

The game started. The Braves took the tap from center. They dribbled quickly and surely. Their passes were swift and accurate. Within thirty seconds they sank the first basket. Before the minute was up, they sank another.

Rusty watched the game from the bench. The Braves looked as courageous as their name suggested. By the end of the first quarter they were leading, 17 to 9.

Rusty noticed how much more action there was in this game than the ones they had played in the barn. It frightened him. How could he, slow as he was, play with such fast players? He wouldn't have a chance!

And then he heard his name. He turned, his heart beating rapidly.

"Rusty! Report to the ref! Tell him you're going in in place of Mark!"

9

RUSTY played forward with Joby. Corny Moon and Bud Farris played guard. Jim Bush was at center. He was taking Perry's place.

It was the Lakers' out near their own basket. Corny passed the ball from out of bounds to Bud. Bud dribbled a couple of steps and shot a quick pass to Joby, who was running toward the basket. Joby caught the ball and leaped. A Braves man jumped, slapped the ball, and it squirted from Joby's hands.

Rusty caught it!

What shall I do with it? he thought,

standing as if paralyzed. The ball had bounced to him unexpectedly.

"Shoot, Rusty! Shoot!" someone yelled.

He was near the corner, just about in the same position from where he had practiced taking shots at home and in the big barn.

A Braves player bounded forward. He swung his arms wildly in front of Rusty. Rusty tried to feint to the left, and then to the right. The player bobbed up and down in front of him like a puppet.

Rusty leaped as high as he could, and that wasn't high. He flipped the ball with his wrists toward the basket. It sailed in a high arc, struck the rim, and bounced up into the air. Then it dropped — right through the net!

A roar burst from the Lakers fans. "Thataboy, Rusty!"

Rusty's heart melted. All at once his fright was gone. He had done it. He had made his first basket in a real game.

The Braves' ball. They moved it down-court quickly. Rusty trotted after them. He tried to hurry and felt his toes scraping the floor. Those legs! You'd think they were against anything he wanted to do!

The Braves player shot a pass across the court. Another Braves player caught it, feinted Corny Moon out of position, then broke fast for the basket. Just as he leaped to try a lay-up, Bud hit his wrist.

Freeeee-e-et!

"Two shots!" said the referee. He held up two fingers, Bud's number.

Bud shook his head discouragingly. He held up his hand to show he was the offender.

The Braves man sank the first shot, missed the second. Jim Bush caught the rebound, zipped a pass to Bud. Bud dribbled the ball up-court. He bounce-passed to Rusty. Rusty passed it back to him, then hurried to his corner spot. He hoped the ball would be passed to him. But his man guarded him well. No one dared to pass it.

Corny tried a set shot from the opposite corner. He missed. Jim and the Braves center leaped for the rebound. They both came down together with the ball gripped tightly in their hands.

Freeee-e-et! Jump ball.

A Braves man took the tap, passed to a teammate. Once again the ball zipped quickly in the other direction. Just as Rusty let out a sigh of disappointment, a player accidentally kicked his right foot.

The player was Rusty's man. He stumbled forward, but regained his balance hurriedly.

The kick knocked Rusty off balance, too. Rusty fell. He struck the floor with his hip, then skidded and rolled over.

Again the whistle.

"Tripping!" shouted the referee, pointing at the Braves player. "You shoot one!" he said to Rusty.

Rusty stared, wide-eyed, as he rose to his feet.

The Braves players shouted something at the referee. They didn't like that call.

"Hurt, Rusty?" Joby asked, running forward.

"No. I'm all right," said Rusty. *I wouldn't call that a foul, though. It was an accident.*

He stepped to the free-throw line, and rubbed his hip.

The referee waited till the players were ready on each side of the free-throw lane, then handed the ball to Rusty. "One shot," he repeated.

Nervously, Rusty took the ball. He bounced it a few times, then looked long and carefully at the basket. A hushed silence fell upon the big gym.

Rusty shot. The ball hit the rim, rolled around it, and fell off!

A half a dozen pairs of hands reached up for the rebound. Jim Bush got it. In the next instant someone knocked it out of his hands. It bounced across the floor. Rusty hurried after it, scooped it up. A tall, broad-shouldered Braves player reached it a moment later. He wrapped his arm around the ball and tried to whip it out of Rusty's hands.

Rusty held on as tightly as he could. The Braves player was strong. He practically picked Rusty off his feet and swung him around the floor! Rusty fell, but he still held on to the ball. The Braves player bent on one knee beside Rusty, and looked at Rusty unbelievingly.

The Lakers fans roared out in laughter: "That's the boy, Rusty! Don't let him take it from you!"

Jump ball. The Braves player won his argument this time. He outjumped Rusty easily. Ten seconds later the Braves scored a basket. The buzzer sounded. Mark and Perry came back into the game. Rusty and Jim went out.

They sat on the bench beside Coach

Alec Daws. Their faces glistened with perspiration.

"How do you feel, Rusty?" asked Alec.

Rusty's chest rose and fell as he breathed. "Okay!" he said.

Alec grinned. "You did fine," he said. "In the second half, we'll let you go in again."

Rusty smiled. "Thank you!"

"But keep out of those scrambles," warned Alec. "Get in one intentionally, and you're out. Remember that!"

Rusty nodded. A little while later the buzzer sounded, ending the first half.

10

THE score was 26-19, in favor of the Braves, as the second half started.

Rusty was impressed by Perry. He watched Perry's every move. There was no doubt that Perry was the best player on the Lakers team. Perhaps, at this moment, the best player on the floor.

Thoughts ran through Rusty's mind as he watched Perry catch passes, make fast breaks, and leap for lay-ups. Perry went up high, as if he had springs in his legs.

Maybe I could have been like him, thought Rusty. If the disease hadn't struck me, I might be out there on the floor this very minute, running and dribbling and shooting, just as Perry is doing.

It was funny how polio could change a person. *I'm well now. Yet I'm not well. I feel healthy and strong, yet I cannot do the many things other boys my age can do.*

His stomach tightened into a knot.

He'd never be like those other boys again. Never.

A loud cheer from the Lakers fans brought Rusty's thoughts back to the game. He saw Corny running up-court with a proud smile on his face, and knew Corny must have sunk one.

The electric scoreboard flashed the score: VISITORS — 21; HOME — 26.

The gap was closing.

"Okay, Rusty," said Alec. "Go in the

minute the ball is dead. Remember, don't rush. Keep out when there's a scramble for the ball. Ted, in for Bud."

Rusty wished Alec wouldn't warn him all the time. *He treats me as if I'm a little boy of four or five. I don't want pity! I can take care of myself!*

When he got into the game he remembered Alec's warning. He didn't want to do anything against Alec's wishes, anything that would give Alec a good reason not to let him play again.

Rusty played the corner. He didn't expect any more than a pass or two.

At last, the first one came. It was from Ted Stone, who was being pressed by two Braves players.

Rusty caught the pass, aimed for the basket, and shot.

In!

A thunderous roar sprang from the Lakers fans. "Nice eye, Rusty! That's the way to sink 'em!"

Later, there was a scramble for the ball near him. It was impossible for him to get out of the way, so he tried for the ball himself. He was pushed, shoved, and almost got his hands on the ball. A quicker pair of hands snapped it up. Hands belonging to a Braves player.

I would've had it if I weren't so slow!

The quarter ended. Alec put Mark back into the game. Rusty sat out the last quarter, not caring whether he went in again or not. He was pooped. When the game ended, the shower was a welcome, joyful relief. No one was too unhappy that the Braves had won, 48-41. That was a better score than the Lakers had expected.

"You were great, Rusty!" said Joby, as

they rode home. "Man! How many sink-ers?"

"Two field goals," said Corny. "Nothing wrong with that!"

Rusty blushed. It was good to hear his friends talk that way about him.

The *Cannerville News* printed a brief story about the game on Monday. It also had the box scores. Rusty read it over proudly.

	FG	FT	TP
C. Moon g	2	1	5
B. Farris g	3	2	8
T. Stone g	0	0	0
J. Main f	1	1	3
M. Andrews f	4	0	8
R. Young f	2	0	4
P. Webb c	4	2	10
J. Bush c	1	1	3
	17	7	41

Alec suggested practice at the barn three nights a week — Tuesdays, Wednesdays, and Thursdays. On the Saturday after the Braves game, the Lakers played the Weston Jets. The Jets beat them, 51 to 42. In that game Rusty sank only one basket.

"That was a big score," said Alec. "But not too big when you hear what they've been doing to other teams. They beat the Braves forty-eight to twenty-two. And the Redwings forty-three to nineteen. So you see they have a strong defensive team. Yet we were able to go through them for forty-two points! I think that's wonderful. You boys deserve a lot of credit."

On the Saturday before Christmas, the Lakers played the Chilton Chiefs.

"Beat them and you'll have something to cheer about," said Alec. "They took the

Braves to camp last week, thirty-seven to thirty-five."

The game was played on a high-school court at Chilton. The seats were nearly filled as the game got underway.

Rusty wasn't surprised he didn't start. He never would start. He was sure of that. He'd be satisfied just to play once in a while. However, the Chiefs were supposed to be very strong. Perhaps he wouldn't see action in today's game at all.

Bud Farris plunked in the first basket of the game. The Lakers fans cheered him loudly. Then Perry stole a pass intended for a Chiefs player, broke fast for the basket, and laid it up!

Four points for the Lakers!

The Chiefs, dressed in crimson uniforms with large white numbers on their jerseys, grew cautious. They moved the ball slowly across the center line toward their basket. The Lakers used a zone defense and protected their goal closely.

Quickly, a Chiefs player passed to a man at his left. The man broke forward. He leaped, holding the ball high over his head. Instead of shooting for a basket, he passed to another man rushing in. The man caught the pass and leaped for a jump-shot.

In!

A few moments later the Chiefs did it again. Gradually they crept ahead of the Lakers. Perry dumped in two long sets, and Ted Stone, a lay-up. The Lakers were trying hard, but the Chiefs had control of the game now. They led, 14 to 11, when the quarter ended.

Rusty started the second quarter in place of Mark Andrews.

"Keep out of the scrambles!" was Alec's warning just before Rusty went in.

"Yes, sir," murmured Rusty.

He played the corner, but was guarded so closely that not once was he thrown a pass during the first two minutes. Disgusted, he glanced toward the bench. Of course, no one looked his way. He might as well sit down and watch the game as stand here like a store dummy.

"Rusty! Wake up!"

He turned just in time. A large blur popped up in front of him. He jerked out his hands and caught the bouncing ball. Like a swarm of angry hornets, the Chiefs players came after him. He feinted to the left, and then to the right, using his left foot as a pivot.

Suddenly, one of the players got hold of the ball. He yanked it hard. Rusty hung on desperately. If he couldn't shoot, nobody was going to take the ball from him, either.

Rusty was jerked forward. He fell, struck the floor hard with his right knee. Pain shot through it. A boy tripped over him as he did so, striking Rusty on the shoulder. But Rusty still held firmly onto the ball.

The whistle shrilled.

"Jump!" said the referee.

Joby helped Rusty to his feet. "Nice going, pal. You okay?"

Rusty nodded.

The Chiefs player outjumped him. Another Chiefs man took the tap, dribbled down-court.

Again the whistle. The referee signaled with his hands. Traveling. The ball returned to the Lakers.

The buzzer sounded. Mark Andrews came in. Rusty went out, limping.

Alec Daws looked sharply at Rusty and shook his head. "I don't know what to say to you, Rusty," he said. "Do you want to get really hurt out there?"

Rusty sat down. "I couldn't *give* them the ball," he said. "Anyway, I didn't get hurt."

"Oh, no?" The coach's brows arched. "Then why are you limping?"

Rusty shrugged. He didn't answer that one. After all, what did Coach expect? Everybody fell sometime!

"I might be wrong to let you play, Rusty," murmured the coach. "You could get hurt badly. I wouldn't want that, not for the world." The coach looked Rusty squarely in the eyes. "Rusty, I wish I knew what to do."

Rusty stared at him. His eyes dimmed.

"Please don't stop me from playing, Alec!" he cried all of a sudden. "You can't do that! I'll watch myself from now on. I promise I won't get hurt. I promise!"

Alec looked at him a long time. He didn't say a word.

11

THERE was one minute left in the first half. The Cannerville Lakers were four points behind. They were gradually catching up to the Chiefs, thanks to Perry's lay-ups.

Lakers' ball. Bud Farris had it. He dribbled across the center line — and fumbled! *He fumbles so much!* thought Rusty.

A Chiefs man scooped up the ball. Quickly, Perry stole it from him! He shot a swift pass to Joby. Joby broke fast for the basket, shot the ball against the board. Missed!

"Ooooo!" wailed the fans.

A wild scramble followed for the rebound. Perry got it, tapped it in!

Two points behind the Chiefs!

Chiefs' ball. They worked it to their
back court. They tried to move into their
front court, but couldn't. The Lakers had
it well guarded.

They tried a set. The ball struck the
backboard, missed the rim. Corny Moon
leaped, took the rebound, and dribbled
all the way up the court. He was chased
by five Chiefs players, but no one reached
him in time. Corny leaped, made the
lay-up, and tied the score, just as the half
ended!

The Lakers rushed off happily for the
locker room. Cheers from their fans trailed
after them.

"You boys have improved wonderfully,"
Coach Daws said, his eyes beaming as he

faced the eight boys sitting on benches between the two rows of lockers. "It makes me feel proud because, in a way, I'm a part of you. You've come a long way in a short time. You've learned to play the game very well. You've listened to me and remembered a lot of the things I've told you. More important still, you're all good sports. Maybe — just maybe — we might go home this afternoon with a win!"

The second half went along with both teams scoring freely. The electric scoreboard flashed a new score first on the HOME side, and then on the VISITORS side. It seesawed back and forth like that.

With two minutes to play in the third quarter, the coach had Rusty go in. Rusty could hardly believe it. He was sure the coach wasn't going to let him play again in this game.

Alec winked at him. "The right corner, Rusty. Let's see you dump in a couple."

Rusty took his position to the right of the basket, and about five feet in from the out-of-bounds line. Nervously, he watched the game as if he were a spectator.

Presently, the action was on the Lakers' front court. Perry flipped a pass to Ted. Ted bounced the ball to Rusty, and Rusty shot.

Whack! A hand slapped his wrist. The whistle shrilled.

The ball missed the hoop by a foot, but Rusty was given two shots for a personal foul.

Carefully he aimed at the basket. Shot. Made it!

He aimed again. Shot. Again he made it!

"Thataboy, Rus!" Perry yelled.

A little while later the quarter ended.

Rusty expected to be taken out. But he was still in as the fourth quarter got underway. Action increased as the final minutes on the big clock above the scoreboard ticked away. Now the Chiefs were in the lead. Now the Lakers.

Rusty felt himself penned in. He wanted to join in the action. He felt good now. The pain from the fall had long since vanished. Gradually, he crept farther and farther away from the corner.

Lakers' ball. Perry passed it to Rusty. Rusty turned, dribbled twice, then shot. The ball struck the backboard, sank for two points! At the same time, someone bumped into him, and a whistle pierced the gym.

"One shot!"

Rusty's face shone with perspiration as he stood on the free-throw line. His heart hammered as he took the ball from the referee. He aimed, shot.

In!

The fans roared. The Lakers were ahead now — 43 to 41. Rusty breathed hard. He had done a lot of running in the last few minutes.

With two minutes to go, he was taken out.

"Nice game, Rusty," said Alec. "But I almost yanked you when I saw you get out of that corner."

Rusty looked at the coach. Alec's eyes were shining happily. Rusty smiled.

The Chiefs picked up another basket to tie the score. Then Ted arched in a set shot to put the Lakers ahead again. Five seconds before the finish of the game, Joby tried a long set shot, *made it*, and the game was over.

Score: Lakers — 47; Chiefs — 43.

There was a lot of singing in the cars as the boys rode home. And there was a lot to sing about. They had beaten the team that had whipped the Braves!

"No more games till after Christmas vacation," announced Alec Daws. "But don't let that stop you from practicing at the barn!"

Marylou came home on Wednesday, just before the Christmas weekend. Mom, Dad, and Rusty were all happy to see her. It was obvious she was glad to see them, too.

"Good to get away from those books for a while," she said, "and be home again! How's my big brother doing?"

Rusty smiled. "I'm doing okay," he said.

"I'm a forward on our basketball team, the Lakers."

Marylou's cheeks dimpled. "I know," she said. "Mom wrote me. How many games have you won? Tell me all about it."

And Rusty did.

A few days after Christmas, Rusty took a long walk into the woods — the same woods he had gone into with Joby and Corny that day when Joby had checked his traps.

He located the log stretched across the creek. Only now the water below it was frozen solid.

How often he had thought about this log! How often he remembered that terrible time when he had tried to crawl across it and couldn't.

He approached it. Carefully, he put one foot on it, then the other. Little by little he moved his right foot forward, then his left foot. He grew more frightened by the minute. The frozen creek was farther below him. And the log seemed so much longer!

He slid on a patch of ice! He fell off the log and struck the ice below. It didn't crack. And he wasn't hurt. At least the ice was strong enough to hold him.

He climbed back up on the bank, and started across the log again. About a third of the way across, he slipped. Down he went again!

He got up, tried it once more. He wasn't afraid now. He had become accustomed to the height. But he could not stay on the log.

After the seventh try he became discouraged and gave up. He had gotten too tired, anyway, to keep trying. And those falls had begun to hurt.

He turned, headed for home, and came face to face with Alec Daws, Perry Webb, and Joby Main!

They smiled at him.

Alec said, "Hi, Rusty! Joby said we might find you here!"

Rusty stared. What were they doing here? How long had they been watching him?

"Rusty," said Alec, "you're trying too hard. You expect to do everything in a short time. That's impossible. You must take it easier, or you'll hurt yourself badly. I know how you feel, kid. I know exactly." Alec put out his hand, the one with the black glove on it. "An accident did this. I'll never be able to play. But with you — someday you may be able to reach your goal. You have everything, Rusty. Keep it that way. Just be sure you don't get hurt by doing anything foolish. Like walking on slippery logs, for example. The trouble with you is, you want to rush things too much."

Alec paused and grinned. "Come on. Let's get back to civilization. Got a surprise to show you."

12

RUSTY wondered what the surprise was, but he didn't ask. He didn't think Alec would tell him.

Wonder how long they had been watching me? he thought again.

He walked with the boys and Alec back through the woods. They did not hurry. *They're walking slowly because of me,* Rusty thought.

Finally, they reached the road. The afternoon sun blazed in the blue sky, but the air was freezing cold. The boys' cheeks were red as apples, their breaths puffs of fog.

They walked past the houses, and down the long, curving hill. From this high they were able to look down upon the lake. It was frozen over. Kids were skating on it. Their gay laughter reached the boys and Alec.

The three boys walked abreast with Alec. They reached the bottom of the hill, turned left, and walked through the park toward the lake. Rusty's legs ached from all that walking, and he wanted to rest.

Where is Alec taking us? What is the surprise he mentioned?

All at once, Rusty hardly cared about the surprise.

"I'm going to sit down on a bench," he said, tiredly. "You guys go ahead."

Alec looked at him. "Guess we walked pretty far, didn't we? Okay." He looked

98

around, pointed at a bench near the edge of the lake. "Sit over there. Joby, stay with him. Come with me, Perry."

Five minutes later a tiny iceboat with a navy-blue sail skimmed across the ice from the direction Alec and Perry had gone. Rusty recognized Alec and Perry immediately, and his heart hammered. So this was Alec's surprise!

Alec was sitting in a seat with his hands on a control stick. His feet were on a crossbar underneath and in front of the sail. Rusty realized that Alec was steering the iceboat with his feet.

In the seat behind Alec sat Perry. His feet were on a short crossbar under Alec's seat. A strap was around his chest. Halfway between his seat and Alec's, underneath, was a long crossbar with a runner at each end.

Alec and Perry sailed around for a while, then returned. Alec gave Joby a ride, and finally Rusty.

"Just keep your feet on that crossbar," advised Alec. "The strap will hold you tight in your seat."

Alec pushed the craft out and got in. He shoved the control stick forward, letting out the sail, which he had hauled in against the spar when he had stopped the craft.

Instantly, the wind filled the big blue sail, and the iceboat almost took off. Kids who were skating stopped to watch with fascination.

Alec steered the iceboat toward the middle of the ice-covered lake, away from the skaters. The runners thumped and swooshed as they whizzed over the ice.

Gradually Alec pushed the left rudder, and the iceboat circled wide to the right. It tipped a little, and Rusty's heart jumped.

Alec grinned back at him. "Don't be afraid!" he shouted against the hard-blowing wind. "We won't tip over!"

Rusty tried to smile back as the wind pressed against his face. Finally, Alec straightened out the iceboat's course.

"How do you like it, Rusty?" he asked.

Rusty laughed. "I love it!"

"I made this myself!"

And then Alec went on: "How would you like to come out here with me every day, if it's nice? This will help you become strong and healthy, too! Help you to get used to rough weather! Would you like to do that?"

"I sure would!" said Rusty. "But I'd have to ask my mom and dad first."

"Of course!" laughed Alec. His eyes shone like bright stars for a moment.

Then Alec gazed past Rusty's shoulder and steered the iceboat toward shore. He kept looking, as if fascinated by some strange sight.

Suddenly, a gust of wind came up. It filled the sail and whipped the iceboat half around! This time one runner lifted high off the ice!

Rusty yelled. He thought they were going to topple over for sure!

But Alec quickly brought the iceboat under control. He turned and grinned at Rusty.

"Whew!" said Rusty. "Almost went then!"

They were near shore, now. Alec looked again at whatever it was that had attracted his attention.

"Rusty," he said, at last, "who's that standing with Perry and Joby?"

Rusty turned. A wide grin splashed across his face.

"That's Marylou!" he said. "My sister!"

So it was she who had almost caused them to spill!

13

"MAYBE she wants you," Alec said. "We'd better go in."

Alec turned the iceboat toward shore. He stopped it at the edge of the park, near Marylou and the boys.

"Hi!" he greeted Marylou.

Marylou's eyes were bright and shining. "Hi!" she said.

"This is Alec Daws," said Rusty to Marylou. "He built that iceboat himself!"

Marylou laughed, and put out her hand. She was wearing woolen mittens. "Nice to meet you," she said. "I suppose, since you own such a beautiful iceboat, the boys bother you a lot!"

Alec shook his head. "Not very much," he said. "Matter of fact, today is the first day Rusty has known about it. By the way, have you ever ridden on one?"

"Never!" Marylou's brown eyes widened with interest. "But if you'll invite me —"

"I'm inviting you!" said Alec. "Hop on!"

Marylou got into the rear seat. Alec strapped her in, then shoved the iceboat away from shore. He got in the front seat, adjusted the sail, and in a moment they were skimming swiftly over the ice.

"I think she's ruined it for us," said Perry quietly. "We might as well go home."

"Let's wait," said Joby. "She might get scared or something."

Rusty chuckled. "You don't know my sister!" he said.

They waited. Seven minutes later Alec and Marylou returned. Marylou's face was flushed with excitement.

"What fun!" she cried. "I think I'd like to go out again sometime."

"Okay. Tomorrow," said Alec. He turned to the boys. "Stick around. I'll take the iceboat back to the boathouse."

On their way home, Alec told them that he had scheduled a basketball game for the next week at Bay Town. Bay Town had lost only twice so far this season and would be strong competition.

"A week after that will be the big one," Alec went on. "Culbert was runner-up last year in the eastern division. That takes in some of the teams we've already played. Beat them, and we know we have something!"

"I wish I could be around to see a

game," said Marylou. She looked at Rusty. "Mother wrote to me that you were doing marvelously."

"Marvelously is right," said Alec, smiling. "Matter of fact, I have to slow him down now and then. He wants to rush things too fast."

Bay Town was as strong that following Saturday as Alec had said it would be. Their center was taller than Perry, a slim, blond boy who jumped, dribbled, and passed with equal skill. After the first quarter ended, Rusty could tell that the blond boy was practically Bay Town's team. Without him, they'd be nothing.

The score was Bay Town — 11; Lakers — 4.

"Perry, you, Joby and Bud cover him on defense," advised Alec. "Try to keep him from scoring. That'll be our only chance."

The boys clung to the tall Bay Town center like leeches in the second quarter. They held him to two baskets. The Lakers scored seventeen points. The score, at the end of the first half: Bay Town — 15; Lakers — 21.

In the second half the Bay Towners were a confused bunch of boys. The blond center tried steadily to get away from his guards, but had little luck. Perry fouled him twice. Ted, twice. Other than that, the center scored very few points. And the Lakers were dumping them.

Rusty played his share of the game. From the corner he sank three set shots. He was fouled three times. He sank two of his free throws, for a total of eight points.

He had played a good game. He wished Marylou was here to see him.

The Lakers carried home the win, 48 to 36.

It was a shocking loss to Bay Town. A fine team like theirs losing to a bunch of boys who had never played under a coach's guidance before this year? Impossible!

But it had happened!

"Alec said we did great," Rusty wrote to Marylou that night. "Alec has me play the corner so I don't get hurt. But I scored eight points, anyway . . ."

14

ALEC printed a sign and hung it in the store. It read:

BASKETBALL GAME
Lakers vs. Culbert
Sat. 2 P.M. Jan. 14
at the Culbert Junior High Gym
Everybody Come!
It's Free!

The sign stirred up interest. Men asked about the Lakers basketball team. Some of them didn't know that a team had sprouted up in Cannerville.

"Where did they ever learn how to play basketball?" some asked with surprise.

"In the big barn," Alex told them. "Over there by the creek."

Women became interested, too. Most of the mothers of the boys who played on the Lakers team had already seen some of the games. After Alec put up the sign, more women wanted to see the games.

"We'll have a crowd there for sure!" said Perry Webb excitedly.

"We probably will," replied Corny. "But what will they think of us if we lose?"

"Won't be any disgrace," said Alec. "Everybody will know that Culbert was runner-up for the championship last year. Our fans won't down a new team if it loses to a team like Culbert. But let's get this losing idea out of our heads! Let's think of *winning,* not *losing!*"

Alec took Rusty with him on the ice-boat nearly every evening. He taught

Rusty how to handle the controls. Rusty loved it.

On Tuesday, Wednesday, and Thursday nights Alec worked hard with the boys in the big barn. There were a few things most of them still did not do well. Corny still was unable to get his passes away fast enough. Joby still couldn't sink more than one out of eight from the foul line. Bud's dribbling had improved. So had his passes. But he still fumbled the ball a lot. And when he did, it seemed always near an opponent. Ted, Perry, Rusty — they all needed improvement.

Alec put in a few minutes of practice himself. It was fun to watch him. He hardly used his gloved hand. His other one was all he needed. He dribbled swiftly and gracefully. When he jumped to sink a lay-up, his feet lifted high off the floor. His hand seemed to go almost higher than the rim. When he finished playing, perspiration glistened on his face, but you could tell he enjoyed those moments with all his heart.

He probably could have been a great basketball player, thought Rusty. *Not me! I'll just be like this. Slow and awkward. I would never play in a game if Alec weren't coach.*

The Culbert Junior High gym was packed that Saturday afternoon. Many fans from Cannerville came to see the game and give their boys support. Many, Rusty knew, had never seen a game before.

As usual, Rusty watched the opening of the game from the bench. He wasn't worried. Alec would put him in sometime.

Perry and the Culbert center went up

on the jump ball. Perry's long fingers tapped it. Bud caught it, dribbled away, and fumbled!

"Did it again!" Rusty said.

Culbert scooped up the fumble. A pass down-court. A quick dribble. Then a lay-up.

In! Two points for Culbert, and the game was hardly ten seconds old!

Lakers' out. Perry took the pass from Joby, dribbled the ball up-court. He crossed the center line. A Culbert player tried to slap the ball away from him. Perry passed to Corny. Joby started toward the right hand corner, then came forward quickly under the basket. Corny bounced the ball under his guard's arm to Joby. Joby took it, leaped and tried a hook shot.

In!

Culbert's out. A long pass down-court. A Culbert player was there to catch it. He dribbled it toward his basket, leaped for the lay-up. Missed!

Perry was right behind him. He caught the rebound, brought the ball back up-court. Carefully, he passed to Joby. Joby passed to Bud. The five of them ran back and forth in a weaving pattern in the back court. Each looked for a chance for a fast break. But Culbert guarded their basket like a family of lions guarding their cub.

Then Perry faked a pass to Bud, throwing his man off guard. He was at least ten feet away from the basket. He took quick aim and shot. The ball arched, fell through the rim and rippled the net for two points!

A yell broke from the Lakers fans. What a clean, beautiful shot!

The Lakers were tight as banjo strings when the game had started. They had moved about like wooden puppets. Now, as the first quarter drew to a close, they were no longer stiff and nervous. They moved with better timing. They were more careful with their throws.

Tension was growing, interest mounting. Was this the Culbert team that had finished second in last year's championship? Was this the team that almost everybody had thought would beat a little nobody like the Lakers with hands tied behind their backs?

What had happened to their great power?

And what of the Lakers — was this really a *nobody* team?

When the buzzer sounded, ending the

first quarter, every fan in the gym knew that the Lakers were *somebody*, indeed!

"Boys," Alec said, while they dried the perspiration from their shoulders and faces, "you're playing wonderful ball. Keep it up, and we'll leave this town gasping for breath. I heard several of these Culbert fans call us hicks." He smiled. "I think I've already heard their teeth crunching, eating their own words!"

Rusty replaced Mark in the second quarter. Ted went in for Bud.

"Just play the corner, Rusty," reminded Alec. "You might do plenty of good right there."

Rusty didn't complain. He was to get in the game.

Culbert started off with fast breaks. They took the Lakers by surprise for a while. They sank two lay-ups in quick succession.

"Come on!" cried Perry. "Let's crush that charge!"

Perry's spark encouraged his four team-mates to put on more fire. They not only crushed Culbert's charge, they also breezed past them.

When four minutes of the second quarter was up, the scoreboard read: VISITORS — 19; HOME — 14.

Many Culbert fans, looking at the score, could hardly believe it was their team trailing in the game.

Then, suddenly, the play was near Rusty. Joby had the ball. He could not pass it to anyone else. He had to pass it to Rusty.

"Shoot, Rusty!" he said.

Rusty almost missed the pass. The ball struck his fingers. It hurt the middle finger of his right hand. He moved into position to throw. Just as he flipped the ball, a boy jumped in front of him and struck his hand!

Shreee-e-ek!

"Foul!" yelled the referee. "Number five! Two shots!"

The Lakers fans cheered Rusty as he walked slowly to the free-throw line. The noise quieted down. The referee gave Rusty the ball. Rusty took his time, aimed, and shot.

In!

One more to go. Again he aimed and carefully shot.

In!

21 to 14. The Lakers were really moving!

The buzzer. Culbert sent in subs. Two tall boys.

"Oh-oh," murmured Rusty. "What's this?"

Culbert's out. They moved the ball swiftly down-court. The tall boys were doing most of the moving. They passed the ball quickly, accurately. A moment later one of them rushed forward, took a pass, leaped.

A lay-up!

The Lakers' out. They dribbled up-court, crossed the center line. Then someone rushed in, intercepted a pass, dribbled down-court! Another basket!

Rusty was taken out. The Lakers needed stronger defense to stop this Culbert drive. Mark went back in.

The electric clock on the wall ticked on. The Lakers put in another basket, but

Culbert sank three to the Lakers' one. The half ended with a change on the scoreboard: VISITORS — 23; HOME — 24.

Culbert was coming back!

15

"THEY held their big guns out on us," said Coach Alec Daws. "Somebody has to stop them, or we'll get smeared, surely."

They were resting in the coolness of the locker room. No one had any comment.

Alec walked back and forth between the rows of benches, thinking. Presently, he looked up.

"There is a way to stop those tall boys from dunking those baskets," he said suddenly. "Joby, you and Bud cover the dark-haired one. I noticed that he's the better shot of the two. Perry, you stay with the blond. I think you can handle him. Press him a little closer, but watch yourself. We can't afford fouls. Corny and Mark, cover the other three. Anyway, we'll see how this strategy works."

The second half soon started. The tall, dark-haired Culbert player took the tap. Joby and Bud swarmed around him like a couple of bothersome bees. He finally passed off.

Mark intercepted the ball! He dribbled down-court, passed to Perry. Perry's guard was suddenly beside him. Perry stopped, passed to Bud. Bud leaped for a lay-up.

A bucket!

The Lakers fans roared.

Culbert realized what the Lakers were doing. The tall boys put on more speed to try to shake off their guards. Culbert's three smaller players began to handle the ball more often. They took more shots. Most of them were careless ones. They missed the rim completely. But some throws found their mark. The Lakers sank one occasionally, too, but the score was going ahead in favor of Culbert.

It looks as if I'm stuck here on the bench, thought Rusty. I can sink them from the corner. Both corners! I'm sure I can! Didn't I sink nine out of ten during practice Thursday night? And on Wednesday, didn't I sink twelve out of fifteen? Isn't that something Alec should think about?

The score at the end of the third quarter was Culbert — 33; Lakers — 30.

"Rusty, take Mark's place this quarter," said Alec.

Rusty looked at the coach in surprise. "Yes, sir!" he said.

He reported to the referee. At the start of the quarter he shook hands with his man, then played his usual position. He covered more area now, though, than he used to. During these past many weeks, basketball had strengthened his body a lot. Especially his legs. He moved about faster, and he didn't fall as easily as he used to.

Culbert's tall blond got away from Perry, dribbled all the way down the court, and laid one up. That put them five points ahead of the Lakers.

"Come on, Lakers!" the fans shouted. "Get in there and play ball!"

Lakers' out. They played cautiously. Each pass was carefully made. They could not take a chance of interception.

Rusty crept out of the corner. He swung in behind Perry, took the pass from him, and started to shoot. A quick hand slapped the ball down. It bounced high. Rusty went after it, grabbed it, and dribbled toward the corner.

He turned. A man was coming toward him. Rusty shot quickly. The ball struck the inside of the rim and plunged through the net!

Two points!

"Thataway, Rus!" cried Perry.

Rusty's heart swelled.

A few moments later Perry intercepted a pass intended for the tall blond he was guarding. Like an orange balloon the ball zipped from one pair of hands to another. Finally, Perry took the short pass beneath

the basket. He went up, flipped the ball
against the board.

Basket!

Culbert called time.

The Lakers didn't mind. They could use
a two-minute rest.

16

TIME in. Culbert's out. The tall boys had been taken out, replaced by smaller boys. They were fresh, eager. Culbert began to roll.

Fast dribbling. Quick passes. They sank two long set shots that drew a tremendous applause from the crowd.

The buzzer. Time out for the Lakers.

"Screen Rusty!" said Alec. "Give him some shots!"

Had Alec remembered those nights Rusty had dunked nine out of ten? And twelve out of fifteen?

Culbert played a man-to-man defense.

130

But Ted, playing in place of Joby, managed to slip a pass to Rusty. Then Ted got in front of Rusty to give him a screen. Rusty aimed, shot.

Basket!

Later, Perry made the same play. He screened Rusty, and again Rusty sank the shot.

"Good eye!" Perry praised him.

By now Rusty was more "in" the game. He no longer played only in or around the corner. This, he realized, was a game in which he had to participate more than in any game he had ever played.

I hope Alec won't take me out because I'm playing more than just the corner, thought Rusty. *I'm sure I won't get hurt. I'm really sure of it!*

The Lakers trailed by one point — 39 to 38.

Time was called. The two tall boys returned to the game for Culbert.

"Ted! Corny! Cover that one! I'll cover the blond!" yelled Perry.

In spite of Ted's and Corny's efforts, the tall, dark-haired forward for Culbert took a pass, broke fast for the basket, and dunked a lay-up.

Seconds later Corny sank a long one.

Culbert — 41; Lakers — 40.

Culbert's out. The tall blond took the pass from out of bounds, dribbled it up-court.

Swiftly — as swiftly as he could, that is — Rusty ran forward, reached out his hand, and *stole the ball!*

He turned, dribbled down-court, and felt as if weights were holding down his legs. A moment ago the clock had said only seconds to play. If he could get past

the center line, well within throwing distance of the basket, he might be able to
dump it in. If . . .

He crossed the center line. Culbert
men sprang in front of him from both
sides. Rusty stopped, aimed briefly, and
shot. Just as he did so one of the men
leaped forward, struck Rusty's arm! He
fell against Rusty, and both of them top-
pled hard to the floor.

Rusty was stunned. He could not get
up. Time was called, and Alec hurried
forward from the bench.

He crouched beside Rusty. "Rusty!
Where did you get hurt?"

"My head," murmured Rusty. "I — I'll
be all right. Just banged it a little."

The dizziness cleared. Alec helped him
to his feet.

"You sure?" Alec said, seriously. "You

133

sure you really want to keep playing?"

Rusty cracked a smile. "I'm sure, Coach. I'm all right, now. Honest!"

Alec grinned, slapped him on the shoulder. "Okay! You've got two foul shots coming. Let's see you make them both!"

Rusty stepped to the free-throw line. The referee handed him the ball. The gym was silent as Rusty took aim, and shot.

In! The ball fell through the rim without touching it.

"This is it, Rus," said Perry near him. "Make it, and we're ahead!"

Rusty aimed carefully. He was nervous, now. Boy, he was nervous!

He shot. The ball struck the rim, wobbled slightly, then dropped through the net!

"Perfect!" cried Perry.

The Lakers fans roared so loudly the place shook.

Ten seconds to go . . . nine . . . eight . . .

Culbert tried to move the ball as quickly as possible up-court. The Lakers were on them like hornets. Once . . . twice . . . the Lakers knocked down passes. Both times Culbert recovered the ball.

Seven . . . six . . . five . . .

Culbert's tall blond had the ball. He charged forward. Perry and Rusty both were in his way. The blond stopped. He feinted in different directions with the ball as Perry and Rusty got closer and closer to him.

Then he shot. It was a hurried throw. It missed the basket by inches.

Perry turned and ran back for the re-bound, just as the horn blew.

The game was over. The Lakers were the winners — 42 to 41.

Cheers filled the gym. Cheers from the Lakers' fans.

"Here's the guy who won it for us!" Perry cried. "Come on, fellas! Let's give him a lift off the court!"

Before he knew what was happening, Rusty's teammates had put him on their shoulders, and carried him off the floor.

Rusty heard a voice start singing behind him, and then everyone joined in:

For he's a jolly good fellow!
For he's a jolly good fellow!
For he's a jolly good fellow!
That nobody can deny!

Not only were the players singing, the Lakers' fans were, too.

Rusty turned, and met Alec's eyes squarely. Alec winked. There was no mistaking the happiness in his face. Rusty knew it was because Alec, who could never play basketball again himself, had turned a group of boys into a great basketball team.

> *That nobody can deny!*
> *That nobody can deny!*
> *For he's a jolly good fellow!*
> *That nobody can deny!*

2450